# Got Your Nose!

Written by Katrina Mamela

Illustrated by Aiden Sehn

Published 2017 by Little Tree Publishing

To Kagen—My Love, My Life

"Got your nose!" Kagen's Grandma exclaimed as she pinched his nose with her finger and thumb. Kagen couldn't believe his eyes! There, right in the middle of Grandma's hand, was his perfect, wonderful, just-right-for-his-face nose!

"Give it back!" Kagen tried desperately to grab his nose out of Grandma's hand.

Grandma moved her hand just out of his reach. "First I want a kiss! Then you can have your nose back."

"No! No way! Not happening!" Kagen stomped his foot and ran out the back door. "I'll find an even better nose," he said as he looked around his yard.

He would find a super awesome nose. A nose way better than his old one. He didn't want to have to give kisses like a baby.

Kagen saw his friend, Charles the bear, wandering along the bush line. He ran up to him. "Got your nose Charles!" he said as he snatched the nose right off Charles' face.

He squooshed the bear's nose onto his face and took a deep breath. "Ewwwww!" he yelled. "This nose is wet and I can smell absolutely everything around here!" He pulled the nose off his face and put it back on the bear. Charles smiled at Kagen and followed him down their walking path.

There, just off the trail, was a moose! Kagen ran up to it, grabbed its face and yelled "Got your nose!"

The moose and Charles both watched as Kagen tried to fix the big nose onto his little face. "Too big!" Kagen cried as he gave the moose back its nose.

Charles growled. He had found a mouse near the garden. "Thanks Charles," said Kagen as he snuck up on the mouse. "Got your nose!" he yelled. He put the tiny nose on his face. It looked more like a freckle than a nose! "Too small!" Kagen sighed and gave the mouse back its nose.

Kagen spotted an elephant munching on corn, just on the other side of the garden. He snuck up on it, grabbed its trunk and yelled, "Got your nose!"

Once he had the elephant's nose on his face, Kagen smiled. This one was pretty cool!

He took one step forward and tripped right over the too-long nose. Kagen got up, dusted himself off and gave the elephant back its nose.

Charles was growling again. This time it was the neighbour's cat climbing over the fence. Kagen patted the cat on its head and yelled, "Got your nose!"

He squooshed the cat's nose onto his face. It was a bit small and everything smelled super weird.

He gave the cat back its nose and looked around to see if there was anywhere left to explore.

While he thought about what to do next, Kagen threw some rocks into the pond. The ripples brought a dolphin to the surface. He looked at Kagen and smiled.

Kagen was quick, grabbed the dolphin's face and yelled, "Got your nose!" It took a bit of work but he got the nose on just right.

He turned to show Charles but since the nose was so long and so wide, he couldn't see his friend! In fact he couldn't see anything front of him at all.

Kagen walked straight into a pole on his swing set.

"This won't do," he said and went back to the pond to give the dolphin back its nose.

He sat down on his swing to think. He needed an amazing nose. A nose so special that everyone one would want one. Charles growled. There up in the tree was a proboscis monkey. Kagen climbed up to it.

"Got your nose!" he yelled and put the long floppy nose on his face. The monkey yelled and tried to get it back. Kagen covered the nose with his hands. It felt like a water balloon and it covered his whole mouth! He couldn't talk!

He gave the monkey back its nose. The monkey screeched and climbed a little higher.

"There's got to be a nose for me somewhere." Charles sniffed at a bush. Kagen looked underneath it and there was a mole with a crazy star shaped nose!

"Got your nose!" he yelled and plopped the funny nose right into the middle of his face.

"Achoo! Achoo!" Kagan sneezed and dirt flew off of all the little finger things. "Oh this won't work!" he cried and gave the mole back its nose.

A porcupine waddled over to Kagen. It offered his nose for Kagen to try. Kagen looked at the porcupine quills and carefully put his hand on the porcupine's nose. It was soft, not prickly like Kagen had expected.

"Got your nose!" Kagen laughed and put the soft brown nose on his face. He looked at his reflection in the pond.

It was a nice nose, but it wasn't his nose. He thanked the porcupine and gave it back its nose.

Kagen got an idea. He ran back to the house, snuck up on Grandma, grabbed hold of her face and yelled, "Got your nose!"

Grandma couldn't believe it! There, in Kagen's hand, was her perfect, wonderful, just-right-for-her-face nose.

The pair stared at each other for a long time. They looked very silly with no noses.

"Want to trade?" Kagen asked.

"Sure," said Grandma. And they each got their own nose back on their own face.

Kagen climbed up on his Grandma's lap. Then he smiled and kissed her right on the tip of her nose.

Made in the USA
Columbia, SC
08 May 2017